I Am The Eagle Free

(Sky Song)

I Am The Eagle Free
(Sky Song)

Simon Paul-Dene

Theytus Books Ltd. - Penticton, B.C.

Canadian Cataloguing in Publication Data

Main entry under title:

I am the eagle free

ISBN 0-919441-34-3

1. Iroquois Indians--Legends. 2. Indians
of North America--Ontario--Legends. 3.
Legends--Ontario. I. Paul-Dene, Simon, 1947-
E99.I712 1992   j398.2'089'975   C93-091068-0

I Am The Eagle Free (Sky Song)

Published by Theytus Books Ltd.
P.O. Box 20040
Penticton, B.C.
V2A 8K3

Design: Greg Young-Ing, Banjo
Typesetting: Banjo

Printed and Bound in Canada

Theytus Books Ltd. acknowledges the support of Canada Council in the production of this book.

INTRODUCTION by the Artist:

I've diligently illustrated and painted the contents of the story in the hope that children of the Earth will realize the importance of re-connecting their spiritual attachment to the Earth. The carriers of the spoken words, the Clan Mothers and Grandparents, urge us to tap into the roots of our ancestors so that we cannot take for granted all the goodness that the Creator has provided for us. Every morning when we arise and every evening before bedtime we learn to give thanks to the Manitou* for giving us a beautiful day. Thus, in this light, we acknowledge the Air, Fire, Earth, and Water, the providers of life. The indigenous people have been doing this for centuries using sage, tobacco, cedar or sweetgrass smudges to ascend their prayers to the Manitou. Since the Great Eagle is a creation that can soar to great heights, it is revered as it is a messenger carrier for all prayers.

This story is dedicated to the child within us. We all want something to tickle our fancies but most importantly, we need to strive for that something extra. It's called Hope. Sooner or later, we're all going to have to face the Truth; that we are here to protect the Earth for the children and their children. The memories of the sweetest song on Earth are dedicated to all who gave their lives so that the future generations can live and understand the meaning of Hope.

With praise to my loving mother, nee Marie Catherine Gunn (1916 - 1988), a good provider and father, George Paul (1910 -) and all my relatives. I would also like to thank:

- Mr. Andrew Maracle, and Elder Mohawk Statesman and Orator for his wisdom and kindness in sharing the story with me;
- Ms. Shawn L. Grey, my daughter, Sage, and my son, Denesee, for their love and patience in the deepest sense.

All my relations,
Marci cho
Ne' A Whe,

Simon Paul-Dene

* "Manitou" is a Cree word which refers to the concept of Creator

Countless summers ago, creatures from the four directions of Mother Earth would gather to honor their future generations at a meeting place which we know today as the Toronto Islands.

From the North, there were the four-legged creatures.

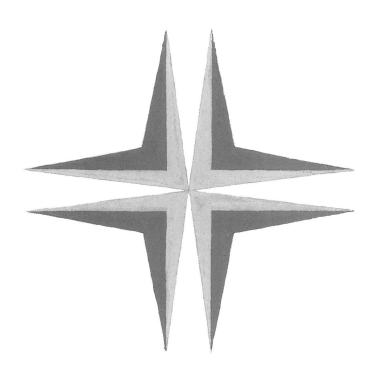

From the East, there were the winged ones.

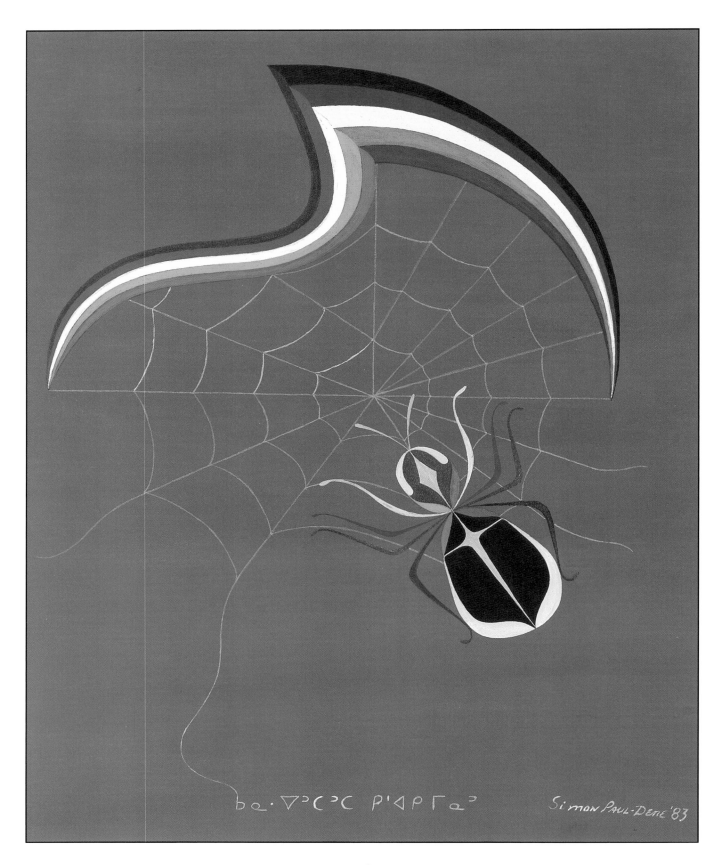

ᐳᐁ·ᐁᐳᑕᐳᑕ ᑭᐧᐊᑭᒐᓇᐦ   *Simon Paul-Dene '83*

8

From the South, there were the creatures that crawl.

And from the West, the White Bison who was chosen to be the leader of the meeting place.

One day the winged creatures held a contest to see who could soar to the greatest heights and sing the sweetest song in flight.

14

The Brother Sun waited and watched for a great event to unfold.

He made everyone happy to be alive.

Even the great Grandmother Moon looked on sleepily.

As the creatures sang their honor song, everyone danced to the heartbeat rhythm of the wings in flight.

The fish in the waters heard the music and danced.

When the song ended, every winged one took flight to meet with the Thunderbird, the protector of them all.

Soon all the birds bowed out of the contest except for one tiny bird who hid beneath the furrows of the great Eagle's tailfeathers.

26

The Eagle glided like there was no end to the sky, unaware of his little traveller.

He flew higher and higher as if he were going to greet the Brother Sun.

30

Mother Earth stood still while the tiny bird sang its song. It was the sweetest song anyone had ever heard.

When he realized how high the Eagle had flown, he became very frightened. He cried, "Let me down, Brother Eagle, Let me down please! I have tricked everyone for which I surely must pay."

MOTHER TONGUE *page 21*   SIMON PAUL-DENE ©91

The surprised Eagle let the bird down to earth gently.

The bird flew away sheepishly to hide in the nearest tree.

To this very day you can still hear its sweetest song, but the bird can never be seen.

36